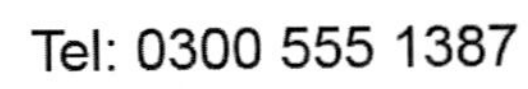

To Mary and Pete (grandparents from Bedford) – M.R.

For Grandma Eileen and Nanny Pat – F.B.

Bloomsbury Publishing
London, Oxford, New York, New Delhi and Sydney
First published in Great Britain in 2018
by Bloomsbury Publishing Plc
50 Bedford Square, London WC1B 3DP
www.bloomsbury.com
BLOOMSBURY is a registered trademark
of Bloomsbury Publishing Plc

A CIP catalogue record of this book is available
from the British Library
ISBN 978 1 4088 8877 3 (HB)
ISBN 978 1 4088 8876 6 (PB)
ISBN 978 1 4088 8875 9 (eBook)
All papers used by Bloomsbury Publishing are natural,
recyclable products made from wood grown in well managed
forests. The manufacturing processes conform to the
environmental regulations of the country of origin
Printed in China by Leo Paper Products, Heshan, Guangdong
10 9 8 7 6 5 4 3 2 1

So: homework, a bath – and in bed before eight."

In most of the houses in Fred and Nell's town
there's a grandma in charge
and she's settling down
with an,
"Eat up your greens."

"Stop picking
your nose."

"Give
Grandma
a kiss."

"What your grandma says goes."

Meanwhile, on Mars,
there's an *awful* plan brewing . . .
"Look at those ladies!
They know what they're doing.

If *we* looked like grandmas
they'd listen to *us*.

So let's beam them up!
I bet no one
will suss!"

It happens so quickly the kids aren't aware.

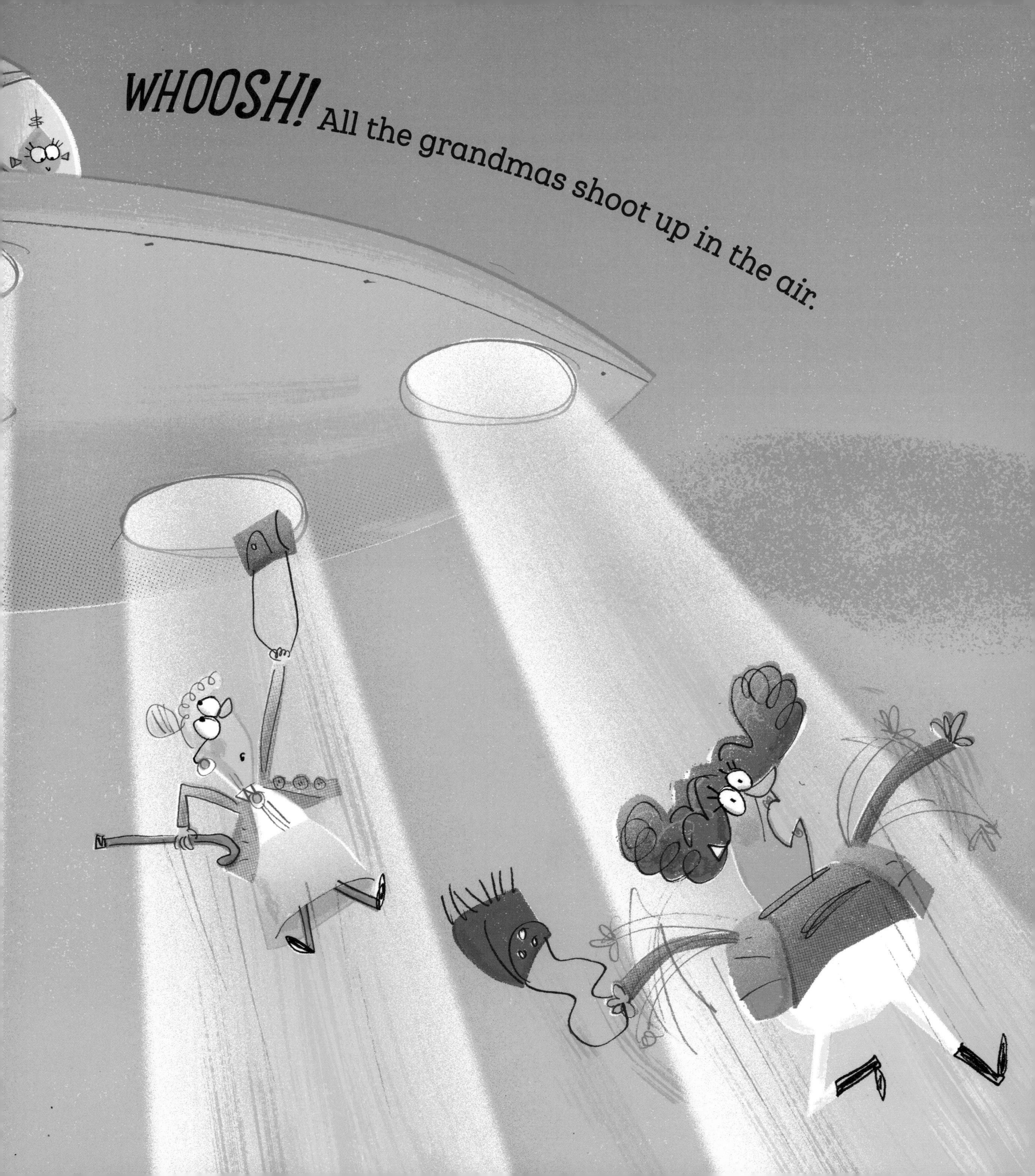
WHOOSH! All the grandmas shoot up in the air.

The Martians replace them
and get settled in.

In place of each gran . . .

there's an evil
green twin.

Fred and Nell notice their
gran's not quite right.

"Eat junk and hover . . ."

“Let’s stay up all night!”

They think about calling their parents but, wait,
Grandma's instructions are WILD –

This is GREAT!

It's chaos!

It's mayhem!

It's fun!

For a while.

BUT . . .

There's something unpleasant about Grandma's smile . . .

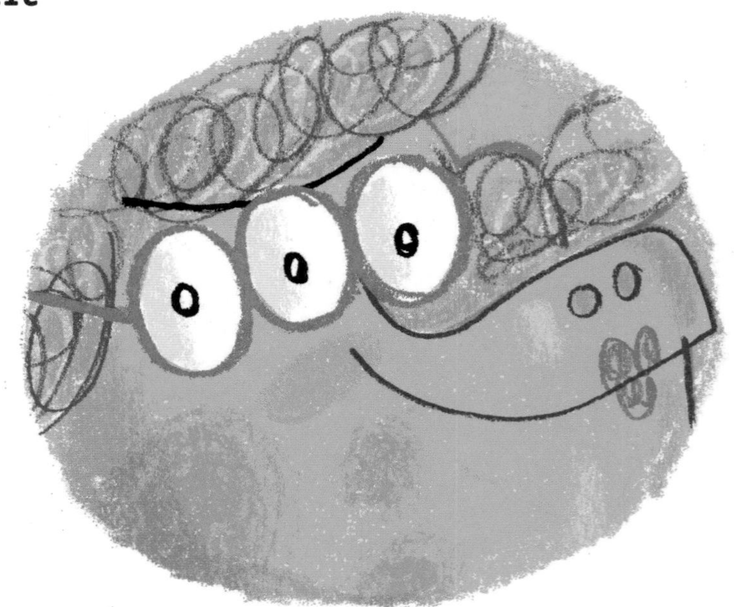

Is that a spare eyeball?

A tail?

A striped tongue?

"I don't think
that's Grandma,"
says Fred.
"Run,
run,
RUUUN!"

All of the children start running away.

"We are your grandmas!
Now do as we say!"

They're going bananas!
They're crushing our cars!
They're crazy!
They're bonkers!
They're . . .

GRANDMAS from MARS!

The town's at the mercy
of little green grans . . .
"STOP SWINGING
FROM LAMP POSTS
AND SHOW ME SIX HANDS!"

Fred and Nell stop.
"This is no time to run.
We can beat them together ...

. . . COME ON, EVERYONE!

They're not REAL grandmas,
they just LOOK the same."
Fred says, "Let's try beating THEM
at THEIR game!"

Nell says, “Good thinking. So, how about this:
we each grab a grandma . . .

and
give her
a KISS.”

It's one thing to say it, another to do it.
But Earth is at stake
and that's all there is to it.

The kids pucker up,

shut their eyes

and attack . . .

MWAH!

"That's
DISGUSTING!"
"YUCK! Have your grans back!"

Hooray!

Grandma's home, and she's not even bruised –
just a bit dizzy and slightly confused.

Fred and Nell's parents look round at the rubble.

"I hope that the kids didn't
give you much trouble . . .?"

"Like two little angels,"
Gran says with a shrug.
"Look, here comes
Grandpa . . ."

"Hey, kids!

Where's *my* hug?"